D1229226

Chocolate Mountain Lake

by Sybil Goodman

HALF HOLLOW HILLS
COMMUNITY LIBRARY
55 Vanderbilt Parkway
Dix Hills, NY 11746

Illustrated by Giorgos at GetYour BookIllustrations

Copyright © 2021 Sybil Goodman.
All rights reserved.

This is a work of fiction. Names, characters, places, and incidents are either a product of the author's imagination or are used fictitiously, and any resemblance to actual persons, living or dead, business establishments, events, or locales is entirely coincidental.
No part of this book may be reproduced or transmitted in any form or by any means, graphic, electronic, or mechanical, including photocopying, recording, or taping without the written consent of the author or publisher.

ISBN: 979-8-9851073-2-6 (Ebook)
ISBN: 979-8-9851073-1-9 (Hardback)
ISBN: 979-8-9851073-0-2 (Paperback)

Published by Crystal Palace Press
Melville, New York
crystalpalacepress.com

Illustrated by Giorgos at GetYourBookIllustrations

First Printing 2021

Dedication

This book is dedicated to **the young at heart** who believe in fantasy and imagination, wondrous worlds where exciting adventures begin and anything is possible.

Meet The Candy Friends

Charlie Crunch   Gooey Looey   Dora Delicious

Marshy Mellow

Fluffawiggle Fluff

Lickety
Lickadoodle

With puffs of smoke from the candy corn steam engine, the Gingerbread Express sped along licorice tracks as fast as its cake wheels would go.

Sitting together in
the refrigerated train, Charlie Crunch
and his candy friends laughed and sang songs
as they started their adventure to Chocolate Mountain Lake.

They couldn't wait to reach their new home, where clouds and tall trees would protect them from melting in the hot sun and rain.

"I can't wait to swim in Chocolate Mountain Lake," Gooey Looey yelled.

"And what about skating in the Icy Malted Skating Rink and skiing on Sprinkle Mountain?" others chimed in. Joy was everywhere.

Everyone rushed to the windows to see what had happened. They couldn't believe their eyes. The Licorice tracks had come apart!!

Panic was everywhere. Fear of never reaching their new home spread throughout the Gingerbread Express.

"I'm scared," cried Marshy Mellow as chocolate tears streamed down her face.

Charlie found conductor Lickety Lickadoodle, and they puzzled over what had happened.

Charlie and Lickadoodle jumped off the train and examined the separated tracks.

With a grin on his face, Charlie suddenly had a great idea! Charlie and Lickadoodle worked quickly, and then got back on the train to spread the good news.

"How did you fix it?" asked Marshy Mellow.
"Chewing gum, sticky chewing gum, just like glue," Charlie
replied as Lickadoodle tipped his conductor's cap.

Looking out the window
Gooey Looey shouted,
"There it is! I can see it!"

Chocolate Mountain Lake
came closer and closer.

When they reached Chocolate Nut Station, Charlie excitedly jumped off the train and was greeted happily by the Raven Raysen Cheerleaders.

Waving goodbye to conductor Lickadoodle,
Charlie Crunch, Gooey Looey and their friends ran
cheering down the candy cane coconut path.

With toot toots from the candy corn steam engine, the Gingerbread Express slowly left the station.

At the end of the path, the candy friends
gazed at the beauty of their new home,
eager to start their new lives at
Chocolate Mountain Lake.

From The Author

I hope you enjoyed reading **Chocolate Mountain Lake** as much as I enjoyed writing it!

If you did, it would be great if you could leave a short review. Reviews let others know whether they or their kids or grandkids might enjoy the book. And your feedback gives me great ideas for making my next books the best they can be!

Review Chocolate Mountain Lake Here:

https://www.amazon.com/review/create-review?asin=B09R3DJW1V

Thanks for reading, and I can't wait to hear your thoughts!

- Sybil

Keep Up With The Candy Friends!

Subscribe to my author newsletter for news and updates on new books in the series, and to get **FREE downloadable coloring pages** of the Candy Friends!

Get Free Coloring Pages Here:

CrystalPalacePress.com/free-stuff